RUNAWAY DREIDEL!

LESLÉA NEWMAN

Illustrated by
KYRSTEN BROOKER

SQUARE FISH

Henry Holt and Company

SQUARE
FISH

An Imprint of Holtzbrinck Publishers

Library of Congress Cataloging-in-Publication Data
Newman, Lesléa.
Runaway dreidel! / by Lesléa Newman; illustrated by Kyrsten Brooker.
Summary: In this rhyming tale in the style of "The Night Before Christmas,"
a family's preparations for Chanukah are disrupted by a wildly spinning
dreidel. [1. Hanukkah—Fiction. 2. Dreidel (Game)—Fiction. 3. Stories in
rhyme.]
I. Brooker, Kyrsten, ill. II. Title.
PZ8.3.N4655 Ru 2002 [E]—dc21 2001005801

ISBN-13: 978-0-312-37142-5 / ISBN-10: 0-312-37142-X
Originally published in the United States by Henry Holt and Company, LLC
First Square Fish Edition: October 2007
10 9 8 7 6 5 4 3 2 1
www.squarefishbooks.com

The artist used oil paint and cut paper on gessoed watercolor paper to create the
illustrations for this book.

For my parents,
with love and latkes
−L. N.

For Rosie, of course
−K. B.

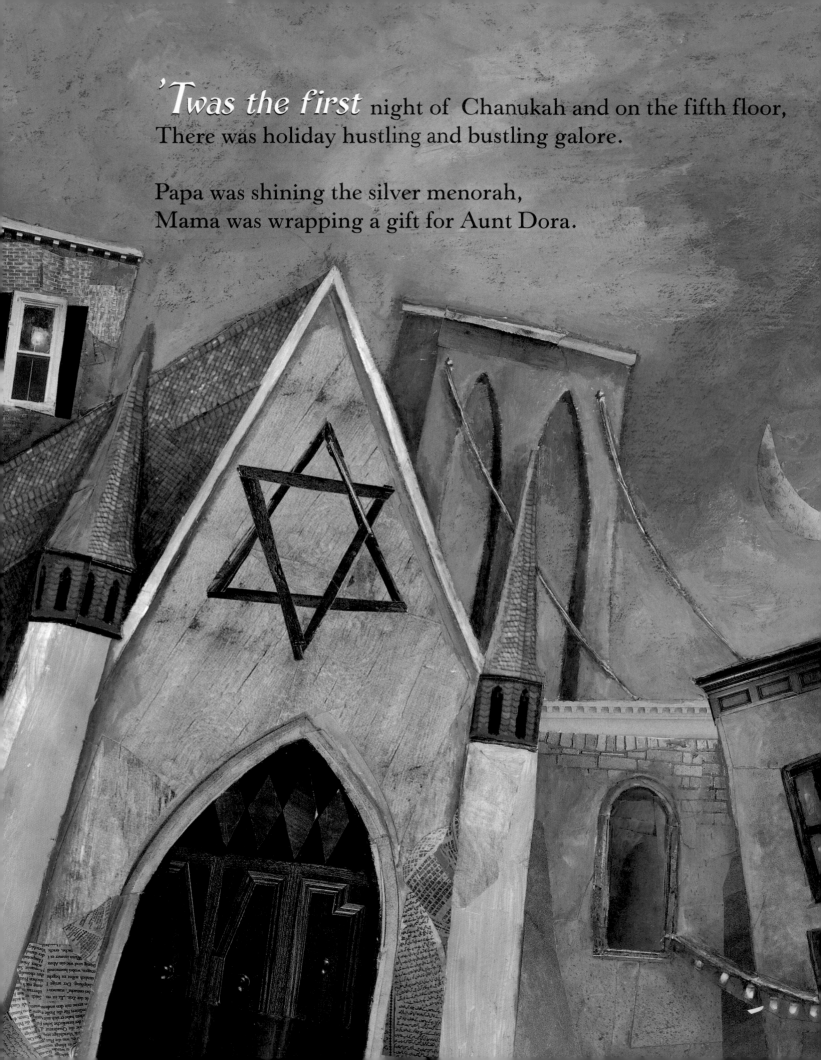

'Twas the first night of Chanukah and on the fifth floor,
There was holiday hustling and bustling galore.

Papa was shining the silver menorah,
Mama was wrapping a gift for Aunt Dora.

Grandma was slicing up two chocolate babkas,
Grandpa was grating potatoes for latkes.

Sister was stirring the soup with a ladle,
And I at her feet spun my shiny new dreidel.

Each letter flew by: nun, gimel, hey, shin,
It was making me dizzy to see them all spin.

So I reached out my fingers
 to grab my new top,
But that silly old dreidel,
 it just wouldn't stop!

It spun round the kitchen
 and straight down the hall.
It spun down the carpet
 and right up the wall.

It spun through the bathroom
right over the sink.

It spun through the living
 room quick as a wink.

It spun toward the front door, which flew open wide,
As uncles and cousins and aunts poured inside.

"Runaway dreidel!" I tried to squeeze past,
But it was no use, for that toy was too fast.

It spun down the fourth floor
past Mrs. Gray's wreath,
It spun down the third floor
past Otto's sharp teeth.

It spun down the second floor
past my friend Pete,
It spun down the first floor
and onto the street.

My family and neighbors all took up the chase,
But they were no match for the dreidel's swift pace.

It spun past the bakery, right by the challah
The baker was selling cheap, two for a dollar.
It spun past the grocer who gave us a treat
To keep up our strength as we raced down the street.

It spun past a shoe store and past a boutique,
It spun past two delis, one kosher, one Greek.

It spun over a taxi and under a truck,
A cop tried to stop it, but she had no luck.

It spun out of the city . . .

. . . and on down the road,

Out into the country,
it never once slowed.

It spun past a barn, a horse, and a cow,
We kept up the chase, we couldn't stop now.

It spun through a forest, past hundreds of trees,
It just wouldn't stop even though I said *please*.

It spun through a valley, an inch out of reach,
It spun through a clearing, then onto a beach.

I ran after my dreidel, my feet in the sand,
In a minute my toy would be safe in my hand.

But that dreidel just kept up its dizzying motion,
It spun through the water, right over the ocean.

And then in a wink and a blink of an eye,
My dreidel had spun itself up to the sky!

It spun past the planets, it spun past the stars,
At last it stopped spinning a stone's throw from Mars.

It sparkled and glittered and twinkled and shone,
Like a jewel in the crown of a queen on a throne.

We stared at my dreidel, our jaws all gone slack,
Until Mama said it was time to turn back.

At home we ate latkes and lit the menorah,
And then just for fun we all danced the hora.

We opened our presents and ate chocolate gelt.
It was then that we noticed how tired we felt.

My uncles and cousins and aunts turned to go,
So we walked them outside to the street down below,

Where we said, standing under a star shining bright,
"Happy Chanukah to all, and to all a good night."